MUNGO
Lost and alone

Written by Jillian Harker
Illustrated by Louise Gardner

Deep in the jungle, Mungo was trying
to slip off through the trees.

"Mungo, tell me where you're going, please,"
called Mom.
"What are you planning to do today?"

"I'm just going to play," smiled Mungo.

"Okay," said Mom.
"But no monkey business!"

Elephant was enjoying a peaceful drink,
when Mungo crept up and yelled,
"Hi, Elephant!

Want to play?"

Then he added, "I know a good game."

"Oh, yes?" said Elephant suspiciously. "What's its name?"

"Funny faces!" said Mungo.
"What do you say?"
"I'm not sure," said Elephant.
"I don't know how to play."

"Easy" said Mungo. "All you have to do, is pull a funny face. Look, I'll show you."

And he took hold of Elephant's trunk.

Mungo wound Elephant's trunk round and round
and slipped the end through.
He pulled it into a knot.

"Wow, Elephant!" he giggled.

"What a funny face you've got!"

"Hey!" gurgled Elephant. "How do I get out of this?"

But Mungo was gone!

Down by the river bank,
Crocodile was trying to nap,
when Mungo jumped out of the trees,
and gave his nose a tap.

"Want to play?" Mungo asked.
"I know a good game."

"Really?" said Crocodile,
suspiciously.
"What's its name?"

"Funny Faces," said Mungo.
"What do you say?"
"I'm not sure," said Crocodile.
"I don't know how to play."

"Easy," said Mungo. "All you have to do,
is pull a funny face. Look, I'll show you."

And he took hold of Crocodile's jaws.

Mungo pulled on one jaw, and pushed on the other.
Then he jammed them both together.

"Hey, Croc!" he giggled.
"That's a really funny face!"
"Help!" choked Crocodile. "How do I get out of this?"

But Mungo was gone!

Lion was trying to
have a laze in the sun,
when Mungo swung down and asked,
"Want some fun?" Then he
added, "Come on. I know a good game."

"Yeah?" said Lion, suspiciously.
"What's its name?"

"Funny Faces,
said Mungo.
"What do
you say?"
"I'm not sure," said Lion.
"I don't know how to play."

"Easy," said Mungo.
"All you have to do, is pull a
funny face. Look, I'll show you."

And he took hold of
Lion's bottom lip.

Mungo pulled the lip up over Lion's nose.
"You see," he said, "that's the way it goes."

Then he ran off, smiling, through the trees.
"Forget what Mom said," thought Mungo.
"I'll do as I please."
He swung through the branches, but, after a while,
Mungo's face lost its smile.

"I don't know where I am!" he wailed.

"That's a funny face," said Elephant.
"He wins the game for sure."
"You're right," laughed Lion.
"Come on, Mungo, give us more."

"Well, shall we help him?" Lion roared.
"What do you think?"

"I'm not sure," said Elephant.
"He did disturb my drink."

"And he woke me up," Crocodile complained,
"which really wasn't fun."

"He wrecked my rest, too," Lion said.
"You're not the only one."

"If we agree to help, Mungo,"
the animals all said. "Then no more funny faces.
Can you get that into your head?"

Mungo looked much happier than he'd
done in quite a while.
"No more tricks!" Mungo promised,
and he thanked each of the three.
"Being lost and alone
wasn't any fun for me!"